# INCH AND ROLY

## and the Very Small Hiding Place

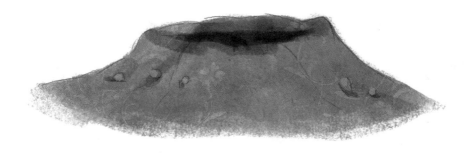

by Melissa Wiley
illustrated by Ag Jatkowska

READY-TO-READ

Simon Spotlight
New York London Toronto Sydney New Delhi

For Lisa Jones
—M. W.


For Michal and Eddie,
two loves of my life
—A. J.

 SIMON SPOTLIGHT
An imprint of Simon & Schuster Children's Publishing Division
1230 Avenue of the Americas, New York, New York 10020
Text copyright © 2012 by Melissa Anne Peterson
Illustrations copyright © 2012 by Ag Jatkowska
SIMON SPOTLIGHT, READY-TO-READ, and colophon are registered trademarks of Simon & Schuster, Inc
For information about special discounts for bulk purchases, please contact Simon & Schuster Special Sales
at 1-866-506-1949 or business@simonandschuster.com.
The Simon & Schuster Speakers Bureau can bring authors to your live event. For more information or to
book an event contact the Simon & Schuster Speakers Bureau at 1-866-248-3049 or visit our website at
www.simonspeakers.com.
Manufactured in the United States of America 1112 LAK
First Edition 10 9 8 7 6 5 4 3 2 1
Library of Congress Cataloging-in-Publication Data
Wiley, Melissa.
Inch and Roly and the very small hiding place / by Melissa Wiley ; illustrated by Ag Jatkowska. — 1st ed.
p. cm. — (Ready-to-read)
Summary: Roly finds Inch hiding in a hole to avoid a bird, but as she and other creatures dive into the
same hole to be safe, the hiding place becomes more and more dangerous.
[1. Insects—Fiction. 2. Worms—Fiction.] I. Jatkowska, Ag, ill. II. Title.
PZ7.W64814Imv 2013
[E]—dc23
2012006107
ISBN 978-1-4424-5279-4 (pbk)
ISBN 978-1-4424-5281-7 (hc)
ISBN 978-1-4424-5282-4 (eBook)

Roly Poly wanted to
find Inchworm.

She looked high.

She looked low.

She looked very low.

There was Inch!

He was hiding in a hole.

"Inch!" called Roly.

"Please come out!"

But Inch would not come out.

He said something.

It sounded like

"Mumble grumble."

"What?" asked Roly.

"I did not understand you."

Inch peeked out of the hole.

He spit out some dirt.

He yelled, "I saw a bird!"

"A bird!" cried Roly.

"Danger!

We need to hide!"

"I am hiding," said Inch.
He ducked back into the hole.
"I will hide with you," said Roly.

Roly crawled into the hole with Inch.

"We will be safe in here," she said.

But Roly did not feel safe.

She felt squeezed.

Inch yelled again.
It sounded like
"Mish mash mush."

"I did not understand
you," said Roly.

Inch spit out more dirt.

"Look!" he said.

"I see Dragonfly!"

Dragonfly swooped down
to the hole.
"Inch, why are you yelling?"
he asked.

"Inch saw a bird," said Roly.

"A bird!" yelled Dragonfly.

"Danger!"

Dragonfly flew into the hole
with Inch and Roly.
Now Roly really felt
squeezed.

"Dragonfly," said Roly, "please stop flapping your wings!"
"But I always flap when I am scared," said Dragonfly.

Inch yelled again.
It sounded like
"Bumble mumble beep."
"What did you say?"
asked Roly and Dragonfly.

Inch just pointed up.

"Why are you hiding?"
asked Beetle.

"Inch saw a bird!"
yelled Dragonfly and Roly.

"A bird?" cried Beetle.

"Danger! Make room for me!"

Beetle jumped into the hole

with Inch and Roly

and Dragonfly.

Now Roly really,
really felt squeezed.
"I cannot breathe!"
she said.

Inch yelled again.
It sounded like
"Mumble grumble
mish mash mush!"

"What?" asked Roly,
Dragonfly, and Beetle.
"We cannot understand you."

Inch wiggled out of the hole. "I said, never mind! The bird flew away." "Good!" said Roly. "It is dangerous in this hole!"